Sleep Tight, Sleepy Bears

First published by Parragon in 2012

Parragon
Queen Street House
4 Queen Street
Bath BA1 1HE, UK
www.parragon.com

ISBN 978-1-4454-9325-1

Printed in China

Sleep Tight, Sleepy Bears

Bath • New York • Singapore • Hong Kong • Cologne • Delhi
Melbourne • Amsterdam • Johannesburg • Shenzhen

There was a **big** sleepy bear,

and a little sleepy bear.

The big sleepy bear yawned

a great big yawn,

and the little sleepy
bear yawned

a little sleepy yawn.

Then the great
big bear

and the little sleepy bear
put his head on the pillow.

Then the **big** sleepy bear closed his eyes,

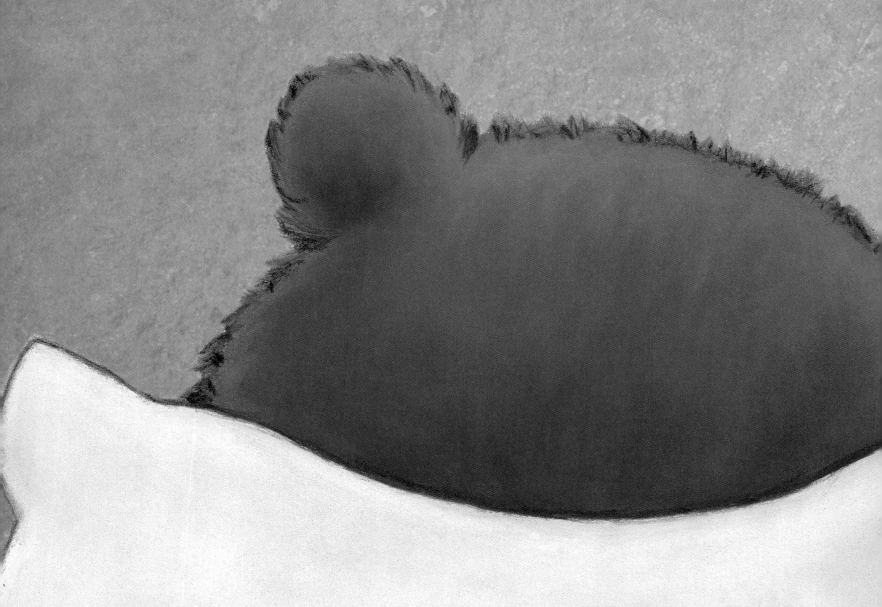

and the little sleepy bear closed his eyes.

Then the big sleepy bear sang

a sleepy song:

When I lay me down
to sleep
Four bright angels
around me keep.

Two to watch me through the **night.**

And two
to **wake**
me come
daylight.

And the little sleepy bear sang

a sleepy song:

When I lay me down
to sleep
Four bright angels
around me keep.

Two to watch me through the night.

And two to wake me come daylight.

Softer
and
softer
and

softer.

And the little sleepy
bear didn't say
a word because he
was sound asleep.